**Put Beginning Readers on the Right Track with
ALL ABOARD READING™**

The All Aboard Reading series is especially designed for beginning readers. Written by noted authors and illustrated in full color, these are books that children really want to read—books to excite their imagination, expand their interests, make them laugh, and support their feelings. With fiction and nonfiction stories that are high interest and curriculum-related, All Aboard Reading books offer something for every young reader. And with four different reading levels, the All Aboard Reading series lets you choose which books are most appropriate for your children and their growing abilities.

Picture Readers
Picture Readers have super-simple texts, with many nouns appearing as rebus pictures. At the end of each book are 24 flash cards—on one side is a rebus picture; on the other side is the written-out word.

Station Stop 1
Station Stop 1 books are best for children who have just begun to read. Simple words and big type make these early reading experiences more comfortable. Picture clues help children to figure out the words on the page. Lots of repetition throughout the text helps children to predict the next word or phrase—an essential step in developing word recognition.

Station Stop 2
Station Stop 2 books are written specifically for children who are reading with help. Short sentences make it easier for early readers to understand what they are reading. Simple plots and simple dialogue help children with reading comprehension.

Station Stop 3
Station Stop 3 books are perfect for children who are reading alone. With longer text and harder words, these books appeal to children who have mastered basic reading skills. More complex stories captivate children who are ready for more challenging books.

In addition to All Aboard Reading books, look for All Aboard Math Readers™ (fiction stories that teach math concepts children are learning in school) and All Aboard Science Readers™ (nonfiction books that explore the most fascinating science topics in age-appropriate language).

All Aboard for happy reading!

For Tom Lennon,
soccer coach and dad—J.H.

Text copyright © 2001 by Rita Book. Illustrations copyright © 2001 by Amy Wummer. All rights reserved. Published by Grosset & Dunlap, a division of Penguin Putnam Books for Young Readers, 345 Hudson Street, New York, NY 10014. GROSSET & DUNLAP and ALL ABOARD READING are trademarks of Penguin Putnam Inc. Published simultaneously in Canada. Printed in the U.S.A.

Library of Congress Cataloging-in-Publication Data is available.

ISBN 0-448-42615-3 (GB)   A B C D E F G H I J
ISBN 0-488-42599-8 (pbk)   C D E F G H I J

My Soccer Mom From Mars

By Rita Book
Illustrated by Amy Wummer

Grosset & Dunlap • New York

Ryan got his soccer ball
and his lucky water bottle.
He headed for the soccer field.
Good thing his mom was
staying home with his little sister.
His mom loved watching soccer.

But Ryan's mom cheered louder

than anyone.

She liked to jump around.

And she always

put kissy notes in his pockets.

That was so embarrassing!

To my
very favorite
son—
Have fun
at soccer.
♥ Mom
xoo
xox

Roses are red,
Soccer balls are
black and white.
I love you
a lot.
See you tonight.
From: Mom
xooxox ♥

There were eight kids
on Ryan's new team.
First they did warm-ups.
Then they did drills.

Soccer was fun.

But sometimes Ryan's feet
got mixed up.

And sometimes he forgot
about the no hands rule.

After practice,

the coach said,

"Our team needs a name. Any ideas?"

Katy wanted Kicking Kangaroos.

Dan wanted Ball Bombers.

"How about Half and Half?"

Ryan said.

"We are half boys and half girls."

Ryan's name got the most votes.

Dan gave him a high-five.

Ryan was very proud.

"Hey, your dad has a dairy farm.
Can he get team uniforms for us?"
Ryan asked Dan.
"They could be black-and-white
like dairy cows."

Dan liked that idea.

So did everyone else.

Except Katy.

She was mad that

her team name

had not been chosen.

A few weeks later,

there was a game

against the Wildcats.

The two captains flipped a coin.

Hooray! Half and Half

got the ball first.

Katy kicked the ball.

Both teams ran

down the field after it.

Dribble. Pass. Kick.

"No hands!" the coach

yelled to Ryan.

Dribble. Pass. Kick.

Katy kicked the ball

into the goal.

Half and Half scored!

Then it was halftime.

Suddenly, Katy giggled.

"Whose mom is that?"

She pointed at the parents.

One mom was cheering like crazy.

She was ringing a big cowbell.

"Oh no," Ryan groaned.

"It's _my_ mom."

She looked like a big soccer ball

with legs.

Everyone laughed.

Ryan's face turned red.

The ref blew his whistle.

The game started again.

Ryan was still thinking

about his mom.

She was the soccer mom

from Mars.

Then the ball

came flying his way.

Ryan kicked it.

Yes! The ball went toward the goal.

Ryan ran after it.

He kept on running.

He kept on kicking.

His team was yelling.

"They must be cheering me on,"

he thought.

Then he kicked the ball.

It went right into the goal!

"Woo-hoo!"

Ryan punched his fist
in the air.

But his team was not happy.

"You kicked the ball into <u>our</u> goal,"
said Katy.

"The Wildcats got the point!"

"Oh. I forgot that the goals
were switched at halftime,"
said Ryan.

Katy rolled her eyes.

"Wrong Way Ryan.

That's your new name."

Half and Half lost 2 to 1.

Ryan walked home with Dan.

"Don't get lost going home!"

Katy shouted.

Then Ryan saw his mom's car.

Ryan ducked behind a bush.

"My mom is so embarrassing," he said.

"I think she is nice," said Dan.

"But why don't you tell her

how you feel?"

Ryan shrugged.

That might hurt his mom's feelings.

When Ryan got home,

his mom gave him a hug.

"Good try," she said.

"Everybody makes mistakes."

"But I'm afraid I'll do it

next time, too," said Ryan.

"I bet you won't," she said.

His mom <u>was</u> really nice.

If only she didn't do

embarrassing stuff

in front of his friends.

That night Ryan's little sister

handed him her favorite book.

It was The Lost Dog.

Ryan read to her every night.

He read aloud:

"I'm lost!" said Dog. "What shall I do?

I'll look for my house. I know it's blue.

It's not by the lake. It's not by the park.

I see it now! I'm home! Bark! Bark!"

Hey! The book gave Ryan an idea.

The idea would help him

at the next game.

It was the day of the game.

Half and Half was going to play

against the Sharks.

The Sharks were really good.

Ryan got his ball

and his lucky water bottle.

He wrote a note to his mom:

Dear Mom,
The game
starts at
3:00.
Ryan

The game was really at two.

So by the time his mom

got there,

it would be over.

"Where is your mom?" Katy asked
when he got to the soccer field.

"She can't come," said Ryan.

"Too bad," said Katy.

"Your mom is cool.
She comes to your games.
My mom is too busy."

"My mom gets mad and yells,"
said Jess.

Suddenly Ryan wished

he had not tricked his mom.

It was mean.

Plus he had fibbed.

But it was too late.

The ref blew his whistle.

The Sharks and Half and Half

chased the ball

up and down the field.

One goal for Half and Half.

One goal for the Sharks.

Soon the score was tied 3 to 3.

The game was almost over.

Oops! Katy tripped.

The ball flew Ryan's way.

"Go, Ryan!" Katy shouted.

Oh no!

Ryan was not sure

which way to go.

Then he remembered his idea.

He had made up a rhyme

like the one in The Lost Dog.

He said his rhyme out loud:

"Go toward the gray.

The goal's that way."

Ryan ran toward the goalie

in the gray Sharks uniform.

Dribble. Dribble. KICK!

The ball went into the goal.

Hooray!

Ryan scored.

Half and Half won!

His team cheered

for real this time.

"Moooo-teeful shot, Ryan!"

someone yelled.

It was Ryan's mom!

She had been there the whole time.

So was his sister.

They were wearing cow ears.

His mom was ringing a cowbell.

The other kids laughed.

This time, Ryan did too.

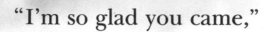

"I'm so glad you came,"

Ryan told his mom.

"Your note said the wrong time,

but I called the coach.

I wouldn't miss a game

for the world!"

his mom said.

Then she leaned closer.

Oh no! She was going to kiss him

in front of the whole team!

"No kissing

in front of my friends, Mom,"

Ryan whispered.

His mom looked surprised.

But she <u>didn't</u> kiss him.

Instead she gave

the whole team kisses—

the chocolate kind.

And she saved the <u>real</u> kisses for home!